THE URBANA FREE LIBRARY
3 1230 00853 3651

D1252530

Sir Arthur Conan Doyle's The Adventure of the Red Circle

Adapted by: Vincent Goodwin

Illustrated by: Ben Dunn

visit us at
www.abdopublishing.com

Published by Magic Wagon, a division of the ABDO Group, PO Box 398166, Minneapolis, Minnesota, 55439.

Printed in the United States of America, North Mankato, Minnesota.
052013
012014
This book contains at least 10% recycled materials.

Written by Sir Arthur Conan Doyle
Adapted by Vincent Goodwin
Illustrated by Ben Dunn
Colored by Robby Bevard
Lettered by Doug Dlin & Robby Bevard
Edited by Stephanie Hedlund and Rochelle Baltzer
Interior layout by Antarctic Press
Cover art by Ben Dunn
Cover design by Abbey Fitzgerald

Library of Congress Cataloging-in-Publication Data

Goodwin, Vincent.
Sir Arthur Conan Doyle's The adventure of the red circle / adapted by Vincent Goodwin ; illustrated by Ben Dunn.
p. cm. -- (The graphic novel adventures of Sherlock Holmes)
Summary: Retold in graphic novel form, Sherlock Holmes is called in to investigate when Mrs. Warren fears that her new lodger is behaving in a very suspicious manner.
ISBN 978-1-61641-974-5
1. Doyle, Arthur Conan, Sir, 1859-1930. Adventure of the red circle--Adaptations. 2. Holmes, Sherlock (Fictitious character)--Comic books, strips, etc. 3. Holmes, Sherlock (Fictitious character)--Juvenile fiction. 4. Graphic novels. [1. Graphic novels. 2. Doyle, Arthur Conan, Sir, 1859-1930. Adventure of the red circle--Adaptations. 3. Mystery and detective stories.] I. Dunn, Ben, ill. II. Doyle, Arthur Conan, Sir, 1859-1930. Adventure of the red circle. III. Title. IV. Title: Adventure of the red circle.
PZ7.7.G66Siq 2013
741.5'973--dc23

2013004375

Table of Contents

Cast

Sherlock Holmes

Dr. John Watson

Mrs. Warren

Mr. Warren

Inspector Gregson

Mr. Leverton

Gennaro Lucca

Emilia Lucca

Guiseppe Gorgiano

London, outside an inn...

That night...
KLMP
KLMP
KLMP

KLMP
KLMP
KLMP

HE TOLD ME THAT HE IS A BIT OF A NIGHT OWL.

RING
RING
Please
lunch
Please
leave

The next morning...
RING RING
Newspaper
RING RING
Match

MR. HOLMES, I LEAVE THAT PAPER WITH HIS BREAKFAST EVERY MORNING.
HE HAS BEEN THERE FOR TEN DAYS. WE CAN HEAR HIM WALKING AROUND. BUT HE HASN'T LEFT THE HOUSE SINCE THAT FIRST NIGHT.
221B
DEAR ME, WATSON, THIS IS CERTAINLY A LITTLE UNUSUAL. WANTING TO BE ALONE I CAN UNDERSTAND. BUT WHY TYPE OUT NOTES?
MAYBE HE WANTED TO HIDE HIS HANDWRITING.

WHY? WHAT WOULD IT MATTER IF HIS LANDLADY SHOULD KNOW HIS HANDWRITING?

WELL, MRS. WARREN, YOU HAVE NOTHING TO COMPLAIN ABOUT. HE PAYS YOU WELL. IF HE CHOOSES TO STAY IN HIS ROOM, IT IS NO BUSINESS OF YOURS.

REPORT TO ME IF ANYTHING NEW OCCURS. I WILL OFFER MY HELP IF IT SHOULD BE NEEDED.

THERE ARE CERTAINLY SOME POINTS OF INTEREST IN THIS CASE, WATSON.
FIRST IS THE OBVIOUS POSSIBILITY THAT THE PERSON NOW IN THE ROOM MAY BE ENTIRELY DIFFERENT FROM THE ONE WHO RENTED IT.

WHY DO YOU THINK THAT?

DO YOU NOT THINK IT STRANGE THAT THE ONLY TIME THE LODGER WENT OUT WAS THE FIRST NIGHT?
WE HAVE NO PROOF THAT THE PERSON WHO CAME BACK WAS THE PERSON WHO WENT OUT.

THIS LODGER WRITES A NOTE THAT SAYS "PLEASE LUNCH" WHEN IT SHOULD HAVE BEEN "LUNCH PLEASE."
BUT, MRS. WARREN SAID THE MAN SPOKE ENGLISH WELL.

THERE IS A GOOD CHANCE THAT THERE HAS BEEN A SUBSTITUTION OF LODGERS.

A few days later...
WATSON, LISTEN TO THIS.
"THE PATH IS CLEARING. IF I FIND CHANCE SIGNAL MESSAGE REMEMBER CODE AGREED-- ONE A, TWO B, AND SO ON. YOU WILL HEAR SOON. G."

DON'T YOU THINK IT'S FUNNY THAT PEOPLE PRINT CODES IN THE CLASSIFIED ADS?

LET'S SEE, MR. G, IF YOU HAVE PRINTED ANYTHING IN THE PREVIOUS DAY'S PAPERS...

BRILLIANT! HERE'S ONE FROM A WEEK AND A HALF AGO: "BE PATIENT. WILL FIND COMMUNICATIONS. MEANWHILE, THIS COLUMN. 6."
I WONDER IF THAT MATCHES UP WITH THE WARREN CASE. THAT WOULD BE RIGHT AROUND WHEN MRS. WARREN'S GUEST ARRIVED.

HERE'S ANOTHER. "AM MAKING SUCCESSFUL ARRANGEMENTS. PATIENCE. THE CLOUDS WILL PASS. 6."
WATSON, IT'S ENTIRELY POSSIBLE THAT WE'RE DEALING WITH MRS. WARREN'S LODGER. GOOD JOB. BUT WHY?

The next day...
HOW'S THIS, WATSON?
High red house with white stone facings. Third floor. Second window left. After dusk. G.
I WOULD SAY THAT IS OUR MAN.

Across town...
HAVE A GOOD DAY AT WORK, MY LOVE.

OOOMPH!

An hour later...

WHAT HAPPENED TO YOU?
I HAVE NO IDEA. THEY DID NOT HURT ME AT ALL.

WE WILL GO TO MR. HOLMES.

MOST INTERESTING. DID YOU OBSERVE THE APPEARANCE OF THESE MEN? DID YOU HEAR THEM SPEAK?

I JUST KNOW THAT I WAS PICKED UP, DRIVEN AROUND LONDON, AND DROPPED BACK OFF AN HOUR LATER.

AND YOU THINK THIS HAS SOMETHING TO DO WITH YOUR LODGER?

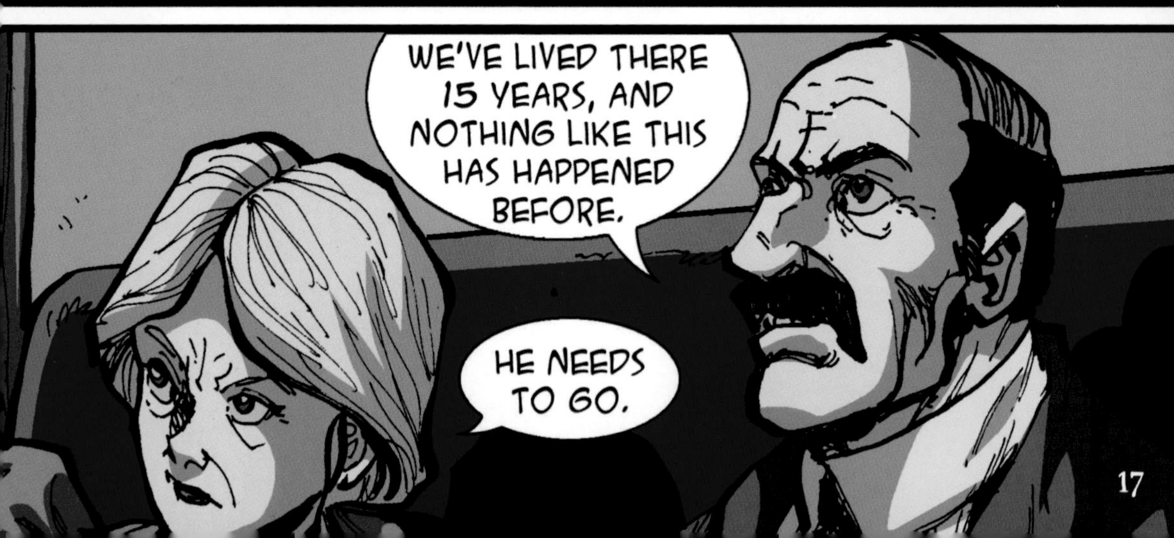
WE'VE LIVED THERE 15 YEARS, AND NOTHING LIKE THIS HAS HAPPENED BEFORE.
HE NEEDS TO GO.

WAIT A BIT, MRS. WARREN. IT IS CLEAR TO ME THAT SOME DANGER IS THREATENING YOUR LODGER.

WELL, WHAT ARE WE TO DO, MR. HOLMES?

I WOULD LIKE TO SEE THIS LODGER OF YOURS, MRS. WARREN.

GOOD LUCK WITH THAT. YOU COULD BREAK DOWN THE DOOR, BUT OTHERWISE, THERE'S NO GETTING IN.

IT IS ABOUT LUNCHTIME, IS IT NOT?

At the Warren Inn...
DO YOU SEE THAT HOUSE ACROSS THE STREET?
"HIGH RED HOUSE WITH STONE FACINGS!" THE CLASSIFIED ADS WERE OUR LODGER!
WE KNOW THEIR CODE-- "ONE A, TWO B" --SO NOW ALL WE HAVE TO DO IS WAIT.
RING RING

SLAM

MY GUESS, AS YOU SAW, PROVED TO BE CORRECT. THERE HAS BEEN A SUBSTITUTION OF LODGERS.
BUT I DID NOT THINK WE SHOULD FIND A WOMAN, WATSON.

SHE SAW US.

WELL, SHE SAW SOMETHING TO ALARM HER. THAT IS CERTAIN.

THE GENERAL SEQUENCE OF EVENTS IS PRETTY CLEAR.
A COUPLE SEEKS SAFETY IN LONDON FROM A VERY TERRIBLE AND INSTANT DANGER.
BUT THEY SPLIT UP. WHY?
MAYBE THE MAN HAS SOME WORK TO DO. AND HE NEEDS TO LEAVE THE WOMAN IN ABSOLUTE SAFETY WHILE HE DOES IT.
WHAT WORK?
I DO NOT KNOW.

SOMEONE IS MOVING IN THAT ROOM.

NOW HE BEGINS TO FLASH. REMEMBER THE CODE FROM THE PAPER. A SINGLE FLASH-- THAT IS "A", SURELY.

Twenty flashes later...
THAT SHOULD MEAN "T".

"AT"– THAT IS CLEAR ENOUGH.

ANOTHER "T". SURELY THIS IS THE BEGINNING OF A SECOND WORD.
NOW "TENTA". DEAD STOP.

THAT CAN'T BE ALL, WATSON. "ATTENTA" MAKES NO SENSE.
MAYBE IT IS ANOTHER CODE.

WAIT! IT'S ITALIAN! "ATTENTA" MEANS "BEWARE"!
YES! BUT BEWARE OF WHAT?

SHOULD I GO FETCH THE POLICE?

HOLMES?

WHERE ARE YOU GOING SO FAST, MR. HOLMES?

INSPECTOR GREGSON, HOW NICE TO SEE YOU.
DR. WATSON AND I ARE INVESTIGATING A CASE. WE SPIED SIGNALS COMING FROM THAT WINDOW.

GREGSON, WHO IS YOUR FRIEND?
THIS IS MR. LEVERTON, OF PINKERTON'S AMERICAN AGENCY.
THE HERO OF THE LONG ISLAND CAVE MYSTERY! SIR, I AM PLEASED TO MEET YOU.
MR. HOLMES IS A LOCAL PRIVATE DETECTIVE. I WAS NEVER IN A CASE YET THAT I DIDN'T FEEL STRONGER FOR HAVING HIM ON MY SIDE.
WE HAVE A SUSPECT HOLED UP IN THAT BUILDING. THIS IS THE ONLY EXIT.

I AM ON THE TRAIL OF MY LIFE NOW, MR. HOLMES. IF I CAN GET GORGIANO--
GORGIANO OF THE RED CIRCLE?
OH, YOU KNOW OF HIM IN EUROPE? I THOUGHT HE WAS ONLY FAMOUS IN AMERICA. WE KNOW HE IS RESPONSIBLE FOR AT LEAST 50 MURDERS.
WE'VE TRACKED HIM OVER FROM NEW YORK. MR. GREGSON AND I RAN HIM TO GROUND IN THAT BIG HOUSE. THERE'S ONLY ONE DOOR, SO HE CAN'T SLIP US.
DO YOU THINK GORGIANO IS THE "G." FROM THE CLASSIFIED ADS?

MR. HOLMES, YOU SAID SOMETHING ABOUT SIGNALS. I EXPECT YOU KNOW A GOOD DEAL THAT WE DON'T.
WE SAW LIGHTS FLASHING FROM THAT WINDOW. WE CRACKED THE CODE. IN ITALIAN, IT SAID "BEWARE."
HE'S ON TO US!
HE'S SENDING MESSAGES TO SOMEONE IN THE RED CIRCLE. THERE ARE SEVERAL MEMBERS OF HIS GANG IN LONDON.
MAYBE HE STOPPED BECAUSE HE CAUGHT SIGHT OF US IN THE STREET. WHAT DO YOU THINK, MR. HOLMES?
I THINK WE GO UP AND SEE FOR OURSELVES.
BUT WE HAVE NO WARRANT FOR HIS ARREST.
HE IS IN AN EMPTY ROOM UNDER SUSPICIOUS CONDITIONS. THAT IS GOOD ENOUGH FOR THE MOMENT.

ONE.
TWO.

THREE!

IT'S GORGIANO! HE'S DEAD.
SOMEONE GOT TO HIM BEFORE US.

HOLMES! WHATEVER ARE YOU DOING?

SENDING A MESSAGE.

A few minutes later...

YOU HAVE KILLED HIM!

YOU ARE POLICE, ARE YOU NOT? YOU HAVE KILLED GUISEPPE GORGIANO. IS IT NOT SO?

WHERE IS MY HUSBAND? I AM EMILIA LUCCA. WHERE IS GENNARO? HE CALLED ME THIS MOMENT FROM THIS WINDOW.
IT WAS I WHO CALLED.
HOW? HOW DID YOU KNOW OUR CODE?
YOUR CIPHER WAS NOT DIFFICULT, MADAM.
I KNEW THAT I HAD ONLY TO FLASH "VIENI" AND YOU WOULD SURELY COME.

NOW I SEE IT! MY HUSBAND, WHO HAS GUARDED ME SAFE FROM ALL HARM, DID IT.
WITH HIS OWN STRONG HAND HE KILLED THE MONSTER!
OH, GENNARO, HOW WONDERFUL YOU ARE!

ONE MOMENT, GREGSON. I RATHER FANCY THAT THIS LADY MAY BE ABLE TO GIVE US INFORMATION.

Four years ago...

EMILIA, IN AMERICA, ALL OF OUR TROUBLES WILL BE FORGOTTEN.

MY UNCLE'S FRIEND, SIGNIOR CASTALOTTE, HAS PROMISED ME A GOOD JOB. WE WILL NEVER WANT FOR MONEY.

GENNARO, WHO IS THAT MAN OUTSIDE OUR WINDOW?

HE IS SCARING ME.

EMILIA, LOCK THE DOORS. I WILL BE BACK IN A MOMENT.

A few hours later...
WHAT WAS THAT ABOUT?

WHEN I WAS YOUNG, I WAS VERY POOR AND NEEDED FOOD. A SECRET SOCIETY IN NAPLES CALLED THE RED CIRCLE TOOK CARE OF ME.
I OWE THEM. EVERY ONCE IN A WHILE, THEY REQUIRED MY SERVICES. THEY DREW ME INTO A LIFE OF CRIME.
ONCE I FELL IN LOVE WITH YOU, I KNEW I COULD DO IT NO MORE.

WE CAME TO AMERICA TO ESCAPE THAT LIFE.
BUT GORGIANO, FROM THE RED CIRCLE, HE FOUND ME.
I WORRY WHAT HE WILL ASK OF ME.

The next day...
THE FUNDS OF THE RED CIRCLE ARE RAISED BY BLACKMAILING RICH ITALIANS. WE THREATEN THEM SHOULD THEY REFUSE THE MONEY.
THERE'S A MAN WHO HAS REFUSED TO YIELD TO THREATS. HE HAS EVEN CONTACTED THE POLICE.

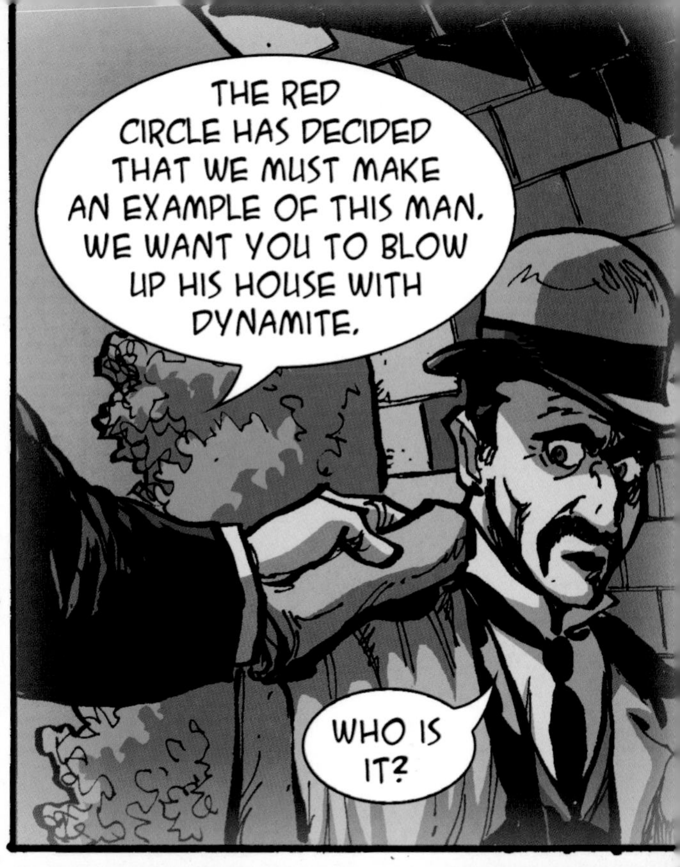
THE RED CIRCLE HAS DECIDED THAT WE MUST MAKE AN EXAMPLE OF THIS MAN. WE WANT YOU TO BLOW UP HIS HOUSE WITH DYNAMITE.
WHO IS IT?

A MAN NAMED CASTALOTTE.
TNT

CASTALOTTE IS MY BOSS. HE IS LIKE A FATHER TO ME.

EITHER YOU TAKE THE DYNAMITE, OR I KILL YOUR WIFE.

IT IS UP TO YOU.

MY LOVE, WE NEED TO LEAVE NEW YORK NOW.
GORGIANO WILL NOT FIND US IN LONDON.
LONDON

Today...
BUT, GORGIANO DID FIND US.
MY HUSBAND PUT ME INTO HIDING. HE WANTED TO PROTECT ME WHILE HE FOUND GORGIANO AND KILLED HIM. I AM ETERNALLY GRATEFUL THAT GORGIANO IS DEAD.

WELL, MR. GREGSON, I DON'T KNOW YOUR BRITISH POINT OF VIEW. BUT IN NEW YORK, THIS LADY'S HUSBAND WILL RECEIVE A PRETTY GENERAL VOTE OF THANKS.

SHE WILL HAVE TO COME WITH ME AND SEE THE CHIEF. IF WHAT SHE SAYS IS TRUE, I DON'T THINK SHE OR HER HUSBAND HAS MUCH TO FEAR.
The End

How to Draw Dr. John Watson

by Ben Dunn

Step 1: Use a pencil to draw a simple framework. You can start with a stick figure! Then add circles, ovals, and cylinders to get the basic form. Getting the simple shapes in place is the beginning to solving any great case.

Step 2: Time to add to Watson's look. Use the shapes you started with to fill in his clothes. Use guidelines to add circles for the eyes. And don't forget to make sure the hat covers the head, not floats on top of it.

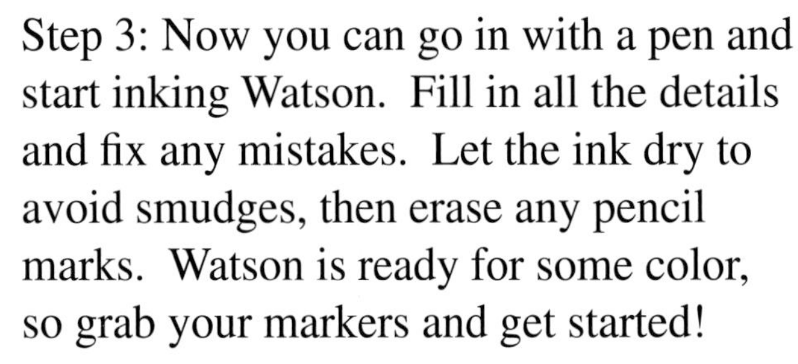

Step 3: Now you can go in with a pen and start inking Watson. Fill in all the details and fix any mistakes. Let the ink dry to avoid smudges, then erase any pencil marks. Watson is ready for some color, so grab your markers and get started!

Glossary

beware - to be on guard.

blackmail - to make threats to tell people of a crime unless the criminal does something for the blackmailer.

lodger - someone who rents or leases a room in an inn.

obvious - easily seen or understood; clear.

substitution - putting or using in place of another.

suspect - someone that officials believe may have broken the law.

suspicious - causing a feeling that something is wrong.

warrant - an official certificate that allows the police to perform an act such as a search or an arrest.

Web Sites

To learn more about Sir Arthur Conan Doyle, visit ABDO Group online at **www.abdopublishing.com.** Web sites about Doyle are featured on our Book Links page. These links are routinely monitored and updated to provide the most current information available.

About the Author

Arthur Conan Doyle was born on May 22, 1859, in Edinburgh, Scotland. He was the second of Charles Altamont and Mary Foley Doyle's ten children. In 1868, Doyle began his schooling in England. Eight years later, he returned to Scotland.

Upon his return, Doyle entered the University of Edinburgh's medical school, where he became a doctor in 1885. That year, he married Louisa Hawkins. Together they had two children.

While a medical student, Doyle was impressed when his professor observed the tiniest details of a patient's condition. Doyle later wrote stories where his most famous character, Sherlock Holmes, used this same technique to solve mysteries. Holmes first appeared in *A Study in Scarlet* in 1887 and was immediately popular.

Between 1887 and 1927, Doyle wrote 66 stories and 3 novels about Holmes. He also wrote other fiction and nonfiction novels throughout his life. In 1902, Doyle was knighted for his work in a field hospital in the South African War. Four years later, Louisa died. Doyle married Jean Leckie in 1907, and they had three children together.

Sir Arthur Conan Doyle died on July 7, 1930, in Sussex, England. Today, Doyle's famous character, Sherlock Holmes, is honored with societies around the world that pay tribute to the detective.

Additional Works

A Study in Scarlet (1887)

The Mystery of Cloomber (1889)

The Firm of Girdlestone (1890)

The White Company (1891)

The Adventures of Sherlock Holmes (1891-92)

The Memoirs of Sherlock Holmes (1892-93)

Round the Red Lamp (1894)

The Stark Munro Letters (1895)

The Great Boer War (1900)

The Hound of the Baskervilles (1901-02)

The Return of Sherlock Holmes (1903-04)

Through the Magic Door (1907)

The Crime of the Congo (1909)

The Coming of the Fairies (1922)

Memories and Adventures (1924)

The Case-Book of Sherlock Holmes (1921-1927)

About the Adapters

Author

Vincent Goodwin earned his BA in Drama and Communications from Trinity University in San Antonio. He is the writer of three plays as well as the cowriter of the comic book *Pirates vs. Ninjas II*. Goodwin is also an accomplished journalist, having won several awards for his work as a columnist and reporter.

Illustrator

Ben Dunn founded Antarctic Press, one of the largest comic companies in the United States. His works appear in Marvel and Image comics. He is best known for his series *Ninja High School* and *Warrior Nun Areala*.